For information:
AF.FORD MEDIA, LLC
15826 S LaGrange Road, Ste. 265
Orland Park, IL 60462

AF.FORD
BOOKS
An Imprint Division of AF.FORD MEDIA, LLC

Printed in the United States of America

979-8-9880203-8-7 (print) 979-8-9880203-9-4 (ebook)

Cover design, illustrations, and interior design by
AF.FORD MEDIA, LLC

haunted house

of poems

Hakeela Buford

AF.FORD BOOKS

To everyone trapped
or who have been trapped
in a place that has overstayed
its welcome
or
was never welcomed
in the first place

Here's to moving on to a new one

Where to go in this neighborhood
PRE-FACE

Pre-face

We are
Just a figment:

Who do we want to be?

Who will we be?

What will we look like?

Will we appear with fire in our eyes in plain sight?
A raging spirit?

Or will we appear in the shadows?

Are we

just ghosts?

The Places We Came From | Hometown

...& Other (Hopefully) Warm Spaces When Everywhere Else is Cold

KEELA BUFORD

Yesterday, I Passed That *One* House on My Old Block

Actually

I think it's just one
of many
boarded up tall bricks
on that
old block

Chopping block
Right on the market
Right on the target
It started off on the corner
And now is wrapped around
Running down the lot
Like an assembly line
For the highest bidder
To be reconsidered
when it's worthy
And to be abandoned when it's
not

Like that Great Fire back in the 1800s
Where promise of prosperity was
starting to grow
And in The Wild 100s
where roses were supposed to grow
and instead, nothing does
anymore on my
old block

right off of 65th & Cicero

there is that boarded-up house

where many souls
haven't slept

HAUNTED HOUSE

Instead, they've traveled
down
that block
like flames
forever in an inferno
burned by
pipes provided by their supplier
or by the pipes that haven't been supplied
heat
or water
for years
And believing that both are punishments
from God
because of what they've done

to these houses
~~they've now made their home~~

And look:

There goes another one.

KEELA BUFORD

They're afraid to come out of their rooms.

Because the warden downstairs
Wants to keep them

there
They're afraid to come out of their room
Because the last time
They were told there's nothing to fear,
The lie
Scared them more
Than the previous

They're tiptoeing to place a foot on the stairs
To get to a place where they can breathe in
Less colder,
Much softer
Than the foot on their backs
And their shoulders
That the congregation
Promises is just a prayer
And a casting away of sins

They're scared
to go down there
Because a knock down drag out
Of a battle of wills and stances
Will push them away
In this house full of soldiers
Who sometimes cannot even discern
Who the lieutenant is
And if that lieutenant is
really just as much a prisoner
of this war
with even greater fear
of the world out

there
They're reaching for the door
On shaky feet
As a state of emergency

HAUNTED HOUSE

mandates
Homeland security
In a home
They never truly had
Such in
And
that's why
The tight control
Is losing its hold

But doesn't let up

Will throw them down
Or throw this whole place down
To maintain these stories
That were told

To feel secure

To not feel it as hard
When the bomb now detonates
Exposing
this world right

here

Got them before
The outside did

And that will prove to be
Even more hard
Than the unbelievable stories
They were supposed to believe
In this house
they grew up in

The Perks of Moving House to House Growing Up

You never got too attached to spaces for too long,

Especially if they were haunted

But one thing about that:

The ghosts still may attach to

you

KEELA BUFORD

Forget the Scary Stories About The Hood
You've heard:

*"There's no rougher hood
Than this one"*

NO

*"No tougher hood
Than adulthood"*

No

There's no hood
Like a child's one

Home
One place
One space

They've never moved on
Moved out from

Not arrested on the street corner

Because they never got
To it

Arrested
On the spot

they never forgot

HAUNTED HOUSE

Only forgot
To move on

But how?

When it's even scarier
Out there
But how?
When there's no other place
Better
To go
And you never learned how
To change gears
And drive forward

And how?

Could you
When you're still only

A child

KEELA BUFORD

When you go to bed at night

Sometimes it follows you
there

When you go to bed
Tonight

Check the closet
Check under the covers
Check on the floor

For what you've been trying to hide
From

But most importantly

Check under the covers

After turning all the lights on
But before running
To get in

Just like you
Check under the lid

Before you get back in
To see if the engine
Is

Still

Running

In these houses we've built

We oust all that no longer serves us,
That no longer obeys us,
Coddles us,
Like a beloved smart device
That goes haywire

By serving a sentence:

Take these words as my cloves of garlic,
Stakes,
Flames
of fire,
Fists,

As my way to say
I'm no longer putting up with this
Come today,
You no longer exist

Until days later,
Or even minutes,
Or even if it's months
To years,

We start to hear...

Whispers in the walls

Laughter in the photos

From the one
That now dwells somewhere between a myth
And a figment
Of our imagination

And our bodies dwell somewhere between
Sweat
And
Tears

HAUNTED HOUSE

Or it's all our imagination...

Like when something suddenly
Starts to ring

And suddenly
we
Realize it's in our hands

The device

That we

Are afraid to pick up
And hear a voice more surprising
Than the one that might've initially
Initiated this
Call,
That might've initially
Been
the true criminal
in all of this

Maybe more criminal
Than this
Call right now
And what might transpire from it

Something that
may
be
the start of something more
criminal

Or
Something that
May
Be
a little bit

too late

With no way to exonerate
From a sentence
That no longer serves us

And
Maybe
Never did

KEELA BUFORD

Why you stay
inside

Once you step a foot out there

It chews you up

KEELA BUFORD

I still can see
you.

Like

The other day
as I
was scrolling
Through my phone
And saw a text
I just knew I had erased

Like

The lights
Flickering
By a single touch
By the bedside
That I knew I replaced

Like
I'm in a haunting
Movie
And if I
just blink harder

And look past the glisten
I can imagine the apparition

Isn't this superpower
That was caused by
you

Because not all superheroes wear capes

Some wear scar(ve)s
That can't be taken off
And disappear

Some wear

HAUNTED HOUSE

ghosts

Like

The one with me:

You

right here

Home Goods

& Other Places to Help Crowd Our Spaces

I'm good

Like
Home Goods
Right before it closes
And you snag a quick deal
That's

Good

Enough
To dress or suit your bed
At night

But not suited enough
For the parents' address.
That's

Fine,

Good.
Like that one song
With the lyrics
They skip over
As they run back
The beat again and again

Cause it's *so*
Good

Vibes only
If only
That could be true
If only
Those good vibes
Could do all the work for you

Yeah, that sure
would be
Good

HAUNTED HOUSE

To be good

Even better
To be
Something
Even more

Spectacular
Like that full-length mirror
You saw in the décor
aisle
Right before
the clock struck

Right
On nine

Right
As you decided to leave it there
Leave it behind

Because you remembered
Seeing you
And everything down that aisle
Outside your room
Would include those walls
Of yours

And because
mirrors can break
and enough bad luck
has broken you

enough

Get Out

Or at the very least

Get out

Of my head

When the maple syrup runs out...

You gotta go back out
You have to

Get some more of that sweetness
That warmth
That wholesome
Stack of comfort

Can't be whole
Without some

And so you
Run

Out

To fill that empty plate

That awaits

Back home

Home Gyms

Are where we oddly push ourselves even harder

The Weight | My Power Rack in the Garage is Wobbly

And I'm not sure
If it's put together
Correctly

Even though
I was given instructions

It's wobbly
And
I'm afraid

To take a chance

On it

Standing under it
Or have it
Stand over
Me

Not because
I'm not sure
of the weight

But because
I'm sure
of the weight
coming down

on me

Because
I added too much

KEELA BUFORD

Home Gyms

Right inside

are where we
oddly
push ourselves even harder
than we do

outside

gyms.

Because we feel safer there

Or don't.

The court at the local rec center has a mind of its own.

You wouldn't say it's possessed
But you wouldn't believe it

Until the court shifted

Places,

The left side
Becoming the right

And the right side
Going left

Bringing unfamiliar
But undeniable
Driven faces
To share the floor with

Or more like

Have to shift
For

So that you wouldn't
Be

Caught in the collision

Of unsolicited
Basketballs

And the ones
Who took a shot

Where you didn't

Move quick
Enough to depart from

HAUNTED HOUSE

Because you haven't been strengthened enough
At home

Home **School** & **Work**

KEELA BUFORD

Schoolhouse (Can Kick) Rocks

Like
The ones
Thrown

At me
In elementary:

Rulers
Pencils

Kids might not be
The smartest
Still a lot to learn
Like how words are
To be written
And other right
Ways to fit in

But they quickly learn

Rulers
Pencils

Are sharp, acute, angled

Enough
To kill

Hopes
And beliefs
And turn them into
Fear-inducing injuries

Scared
To speak
Up

Like one used to

HAUNTED HOUSE

Because
Sticks and stones
Might break my bones
But words
will never hurt me

When the damage
Has already been done

And no spell
Ing
No curse
Of broken penmanship
Can be undone

Etched
And set in

stone

There's a recurring message in my inbox that keeps mysteriously popping back up even after I delete it

Remember who sent you this

No

That message,
while you escape on your cell phone
while on the clock,
isn't Afterpay
or collections
or that recruiter with *that* job
that
just as mysteriously keeps
popping back up on LinkedIn every three business weeks

Much like you get that
Experian alert coincidentally
Every three business weeks

No

That message
It isn't even the subject line of the email

It's the message you see
When you open the email

But the thing is
You actually haven't opened the email

Never do

And yet you know exactly what it says

Why? And how?

Because the email
Is from

you

HAUNTED HOUSE

Imagine that

It's scarier
Than
a missed Afterpay payment,
an overdraft fee alert,

Or even possible identity theft:

Telling yourself
not to lose yourself

Because
You don't remember
The last time you
Delivered a message to
You

While many
Oddly enough
Do it all the time (yes, via email):
To-
do lists
To
pay that payment on time,
To finally create a budget *right* now,
To apply to
that (real) job,
that credit freeze while you try
to
erase
your identity that has become someone else's and

To

Remember

That it is yours to reclaim

KEELA BUFORD

When you accidentally sleep over on the job

You say you're sorry

For
Sleeping
Over

But it's all over

It's time to go

And you walk out
With
Hopefully
At least,
Since your dignity is gone,

A pillow that you managed to scramble
And keep up in your hand
after you tap the Down button
or the Hang up icon

Since
Cents
Might be even more sparse
On the month of severance pay
Than they were on
The infinite months of pay
Checks

Prior
To this sleepover

Where you garnered that third check
In probation
Three strikes

and you're out

of luck

and maybe even those cents
if that package
never arrives

Because we all know
How long it takes
For mail you look forward to
To forward to you
these days

That's why you just went ahead and got the

Pillows
for yourself

In Home Goods
Before you came

House Parties

& Other Spaces Where We're Supposed to Be Happy
But better stay safe, too

KEELA BUFORD

Helium

Places of smiles
And of coming back down
That's the Balloon Museum

it finally stopped here for a while in ATL
to give, well,
balloons
and birthday licks

to my cousin's son who just turned
one
room began with laughter and exploration until
one
swift shove from the swinging pendulum
of helium

and he was knocked down
cried a bit
then bounced back
up and kicked
right in return

Maybe I should've done the same
to the swift diss
by the young lady behind the counter
just before the exit
who was handing over change
in exchange
for the poodles
she told me ever so kindly not to touch
and I wondered if it mattered so much,
then why a sign such
as this wasn't up:
"Watch out, no muzzles"
Since it so obviously had

Jaws of latex
in this house of balloons

HAUNTED HOUSE

Maybe I should've done the same
To the swift diss
of the ones who were one minute smiling with us
and the next, without opening their mouths, putting us
down
my cousin and I

for letting her baby son fall
and letting him

cry

because it's something we're not supposed to do
fear to do
especially to
our boys

even in a place
as safe
and fun
as a house of
whimsical joys

like
balloons

If you tap your shot glass three times...

It appears

Right under your nose
As you pull it down from your lips

You see it

Shot
Through
That glass
And into

The pits
Of hell

An inferno burning right there
In your throat
And traveling even farther down
To the pit
Of your stomach
As you start to hear gurgling
That you can't distinguish as coming from
Your gut
or

It

can only be ridden of by purging it
up

Three times

And sometimes,
Even more

KEELA BUFORD

"I was told I'd be picked up by now."

As the bus rolled up,
But didn't contain

Anyone

Yet again,
You said
Those words

And once again,
There were no words
back.

Because
no one is on that
bus.

The bus
Drives
With no driver in sight

Here
At this drop-off

And everyone that is here
Is here
For the same reason:

To get dropped off
And eventually,
When it's finally time,
To get picked up
Once again

And finally
Return home

Where we left a part of it
Before

HAUNTED HOUSE

Getting on
And then getting off

This bus

For what feels like an extra long field trip.

Except this time, with
No chaperones
And no partners assigned,

Not even a driver.

No matter how unsettling it is,

Before the bus comes rolling back up again,

Don't let this trip be a *party* party
Because then
You might not even know
When it's time to go
home
Over

and

over

Again...

Homes **Outside**

Shelters, Vacation Rentals, Casinos
& Other Places That We Take a Risk on

HAUNTED HOUSE

KEELA BUFORD

The scariest gamble is the one you pass up on

When you're in
The House

It can be a choice between
You
And the you
That stays exactly where you were
Yesterday
And the day
Before

When there are cards
Chess pieces
And dice

That can be the keys

To drive
Forward

Like one of the knights
To seize the queen before the rest

Seize the day

Or
Of course
You can stay

With those cards in your hands
And that set of ten
You never release

Because who wants to see
It fall
And lose one of its legs
Or show its hand
And see
It's really bare

HAUNTED HOUSE

Or
What's really there

And
Of course
You can
Just keep it that way
And stay

Because
it's The House
you've been dealt
with

Four Different TikTok Videos Say Vegas, Lake Lanier, the Appalachians, and New Orleans are Haunted Portals

67

Well damn,

At this point

Sounds like all of them are,
These places we dwell in

But maybe

That's
the point.

Auto Shops are Scary

Yeah,
Even more than that bill
They hand over with a smile
At the end of four cold long hours
When in stark comparison outside
It's reaching almost ninety-nine

Welcome to the South

Almost feels like
Sometimes
You're waiting for a vampire
Or even better a magician
And his hat
To greet you around the corner
Of broke and now
Even more broke

And you can see your breath
Leave your body
Almost like you're still up North

When they slam you
with that bill

And then,
Things get scarier:

There's a bee
That looks more like an apocalyptic hornet
That's been resting over your head

Welcome to the South

But you didn't notice it
because of all the cold
in that room,
and still it survives

But you didn't feel it at first
Because of all the cold
In that room:
A wife

HAUNTED HOUSE

Doing what one does best
Ordering her husband
To order tickets
for a movie
After leaving out of here

That he'll magically pull off,
Pull out
Of his wallet
After wiping it cleaner
Than the large popcorn
She'll surely ask for
Even after leaving this here

Cold room

But maybe her sweet iced tea
twang
Will make it all much more easy
to stomach

Welcome to the South

And wait, there's more:
A four
year old kid biting another,
Her brother,
In the back

And their sister
Laying down the law:
Bite harder

Maybe the kid heard it
Over the scream
Naturally from her brother

The mother definitely didn't
While listening more closely
To someone on her phone
Who had an even bigger
Stab in the back:
A possible layoff with three kids

But the cashier
As I approached the desk definitely did
Hand one over,
and in my hand
it fell,
(not a rabbit)
A bite

Worse than the cold
Worse than the bee
Without her even baring her teeth

Not even
a smile

Home Sweet **Home**

There is a Person at your Living Room

It sounds like a badly written
Straight to Tubi horror flick

But the true horror
Is

it's just me

Being alerted by Ring
That I

Should probably
Finally

Get some sleep

How is your new
home looking now?
Share with us.

KEELA BUFORD
is the author of *Pride, and Joy*
(yes, the comma is intentional),
somewhat like the historical sister novel to her
second novel, *The Buy-In.* She is a content specialist
who has helped many businesses in vast
industries. Her creative and screenplay works have
placed in semifinalist positions with Stage 32,
WeScreenplay, Outfest, and IndieFEST.

www.ingramcontent.com/pod-product-compliance
Lightning Source LLC
Chambersburg PA
CBHW061551310726
48972CB00008B/2710